JENNIFER
AND
JOSEPHINE

written and illustrated by
BILL PEET

HOUGHTON MIFFLIN COMPANY BOSTON

To three stray kittens
the Peet family discovered
on the Malibu road

Printed in the United States of America
LIBRARY OF CONGRESS CATALOG CARD NUMBER: 67-20373
ISBN: 0-395-18225-5 REINFORCED EDITION
ISBN: 0-395-29608-0 PAPERBOUND EDITION

15 14 13 12 11

Jennifer was already an old automobile way back in the year of 1933. The old touring car had traveled over a hundred thousand miles and been sold or traded so many times she couldn't remember all the owners. Now at last she was worn out and sold for scrap iron and left sitting in the far corner of an auto junkyard, just passing the time rusting away. Still Jennifer wasn't altogether unhappy, at least she had a friend, a scrawny stray cat named Josephine.

Josephine had raised a litter of kittens in the back seat of the old car. When the kittens were grown up enough to look out for themselves, one by one they had wandered away, while the mother cat stayed. Josephine had become attached to the car, for it was the only home she'd ever had.

The cat left her rickety old house on wheels just long enough to search for food. She wandered the neighborhood alleys, stopping at kitchen doors where there was a chance of a few scraps and leftovers. Then she hurried home, afraid she might find her old car in pieces. That was what happened to all the other old cars in the junkyard. They were sold for parts, so it was only a matter of time.

One morning Josephine was awakened by the sound of voices. They were very close by and the curious cat sat up for a look. It was the junkyard man and a large long-legged fellow with two suitcases and puffing a cigar.

"I buy 'em cheap and run the wheels off 'em," growled the big fellow, "will she run?"

"You can give her a try," said the junkyard man, "they built 'em to last in those days."

The fellow sat down heavily behind the steering wheel, then jammed a big foot on the starter. There was a "row-er-r row-er-r row-er-r" then a "sputter-sput-sput" ending with a cough.

"Try 'er again," said the junkyard man, "she'll run." Once more the big foot jammed on the starter and once more there was a "row-er-r row-er-r row-er-r" and a "sputter-sput-sput."

Suddenly the old car's motor came to life with a mighty roar! Josephine was so startled she leaped out of the back seat and over the fence. It was a big surprise to Jennifer too. She never dreamed that her rusty old motor would ever run again.

"If you'll take her," said the junkyard man, "I'll throw in a set of good used tires at the very same price."

"It's a deal," growled the big fellow, "if you can change 'em in a hurry. I've got places to go."

In half an hour Jennifer went tottering across the junkyard on a set of good used tires. As the old car reached the gate and was about to head out into the street, Josephine decided she was going too. And she shot across the junkyard like a streak, leaped onto a rear fender, and slipped quietly into the back seat.

It had been years since Jennifer had driven down a city street and she was alarmed at the way things had changed. Now there was ten times as much traffic. It was one great turmoil of taxis, trucks, and autos rudely crowding their way past streetcars and buses with noisy mobs of people swarming in between. Jennifer's driver was just as pushy and rude as the rest and he bullied his way right through the midst of the jam and on across the city. Josephine had an uneasy feeling that there might be trouble ahead.

When they had passed the city limits and were heading out into the country, the man turned on the speed. In a few miles the old car was racing along at fifty, then fifty-five and pretty soon sixty! Jennifer was horrified. They were going much too fast for the twisting, hilly dirt roads full of ruts and chuckholes.

The poor cat was scared, for this was her first automobile ride. The fastest she'd ever traveled was on her own four feet, and both the car and the cat were relieved when at last they pulled into a small town.

The frantic fellow brought the car to a jolting stop on the main street, jerked his suitcases off the seat, and went charging into a hardware store. Josephine guessed he must be a traveling salesman and since she didn't know his name she thought of him as Mr. Frenzy.

In a few minutes Mr. Frenzy came bustling out of the store and in three long steps and a jump he was back in the car and away they went.

As they left the small town and were just beginning to pick up speed, they were caught behind a huge trailer-truck with a heavy load creeping up a steep hill at two miles an hour. Mr. Frenzy was furious!

Suddenly they went charging past the truck on the wrong side of the road. Josephine couldn't believe anyone could be so foolhardy as to pass on a hill. Even a cat knew better than that. If something happened to be coming up the other side of the hill there could be a catastrophe. And, sure enough, something *was* coming!

It was another huge truck charging straight for them! There was no place to go but off the road, and with one desperate jerk on the steering wheel Mr. Frenzy sent Jennifer crashing through a rail fence, then she went careening across a field out of control.

The old car ripped through a haystack, sideswiped a henhouse, plowed through a pumpkin patch, uprooted a scarecrow, crashed through another fence, then bounced back onto the road with a "bam!" as her right rear tire blew out.

Mr. Frenzy was out of the car in one leap, jacked up the rear wheels, ripped off the tattered tire, and jammed on the spare. Then frantically he worked away at the air pump, expecting a furious farmer to come charging out of the farmhouse at any second.

But the only one there was a fiercely barking collie in the front yard. The farmer and his family had gone to the county fair, so Mr. Frenzy was lucky. In a few minutes he drove off as if nothing had happened.

Josephine thought surely the fellow would slow down after such a close call with the truck. However, she was mistaken. Pretty soon they were racing a fast freight train, and on ahead the road took a sharp turn over the railroad crossing.

The engineer warned the car to stop with a shrieking blast on the whistle, but there was no stopping Mr. Frenzy. He was in too big a hurry to wait for a long freight train to pass, and he kept the old car racing ahead at top speed.

As they swerved wildly around the turn toward the crossing, the
terrified cat was nearly thrown out. She barely managed to hang on
by her claws while Jennifer went "humpity-bump" over the tracks
one jump ahead of the engine's cowcatcher.

"Surely a scare like that should bring the man to his senses,"
sighed Josephine as she flopped down onto the car seat. However, the
poor cat knew better.

The foolhardy Mr. Frenzy kept a big foot jammed on the gas pedal and the old car raced on while Josephine worried. They were heading straight into a storm. Billowing black clouds rolled over the country-side, and a streak of lightning shot through the sky followed by a great rumble of thunder.

The fierce wind sent tree limbs sailing past them and threatened to rip off Jennifer's flimsy old top. Then the rain came roaring down, pounding the dusty road into slippery mud. And still the frantic fellow sent the old car racing on at top speed.

As night came on Mr. Frenzy wheeled the old car into a service station at a crossroad. She was nearly out of gas. After the tank was filled and he had paid the attendant, Mr. Frenzy asked, "How's the road to Martinstown?"

"Hilly as a camel's back and all mud," warned the man. "If you try that road tonight you're takin' an awful chance."

An awful chance was just the thing for Mr. Frenzy and Josephine wasn't a bit surprised when they headed down the road to Martinstown through the driving rain. And as the man had warned the road was "hilly as a camel's back and all mud." As Jennifer struggled up and down the hills, her churning wheels began slipping backward, then sideways. Suddenly she skidded off the road, plunging over an embankment into a ravine to end up nose down in a tangle of brush.

Still there was no stopping Mr. Frenzy. He pulled off his shoes and socks, rolled up his pant legs, jerked the suitcases off the seat, leaped up the embankment, and went sloshing away through the mud toward Martinstown.

Josephine was left crouched in a corner on the back seat where she remained while the rain kept roaring down without a let-up.

By morning the stream that trickled down the ravine had become a raging torrent of muddy water. The powerful current swirled up to the old car's front fenders and headlights, turning her half around. Josephine was desperate. If something wasn't done soon her old car would be swept away. She scrambled out onto the top looking wildly about for help, but there wasn't a soul in sight. The only sign of life was a red barn just over the hill beyond the trees.

In one leap Josephine took off across the woods straight for the
barn. She hoped someone was there who could help. The miserably
wet cat fought her way through the brambles and brush, dodging
past trees, bounding over logs, then slipping under a rail fence out
into a barnyard. At first glance the place seemed deserted, then as
she approached the barn she discovered someone.

A small boy was in the barn shed feeding a swarm of fat farm cats and Josephine quickly caught his attention with a loud mournful "murr-ower!"

"Here, cat," he called, "come in out of the rain and have some breakfast."

Josephine replied with another mournful "murr-ower" and headed back for the woods.

"I'll bet she's got a batch of kittens out there," thought the boy, and he left the other cats to go splashing across the barnyard.

He vaulted the rail fence and went stumbling along through the tangle of undergrowth with the scrawny stray cat leading the way. When they finally reached the old car the boy peeked inside.

"No kittens on the seats," he muttered, "and no kittens on the floor. If it's not kittens it must be this old car you're worried about." Then he hurried away through the woods leaving Josephine with one slim hope. She knew that most small boys loved old automobiles.

Sure enough the boy did love old automobiles, and to Josephine's joy he returned with his father and a team of horses. They chained the team to the car's rear bumper and after a bit of a struggle hauled her out of the ravine back onto the road.

Then with the horses hitched to the front bumper they headed back to the farm.

"Can we keep it?" asked the boy who was riding one of the horses.

"It's not ours," said the father, "we'll store it in the barn shed until the owner shows up."

The owner never did show up and at last the farmer decided the old car was theirs.

"She still runs pretty good," he said to his son, "so we might as well drive her into town now and then."

The fellow was a slow careful driver, never going more than twenty miles an hour which was just about Jennifer's favorite speed. And Josephine always went along, either riding in the back seat or on the top. It didn't matter whether anyone knew it or not, the old touring car really belonged to the cat.